Squirrel

RESCUE

Jennifer Keats Curtis

Illustrated by Laura Jacques

Schiffer Publishing Ltd

4880 Lower Valley Road • Atglen, PA 19310

Published by Schiffer Publishing Ltd.
4880 Lower Valley Road
Atglen, PA 19310
Phone: (610) 593-1777; Fax: (610) 593-2002
E-mail: Info@schifferbooks.com

For the largest selection of fine reference books on this and related subjects, please visit our
website at **www.schifferbooks.com.** You may also write for a free catalog.

This book may be purchased from the publisher.
Please try your bookstore first.

We are always looking for people to write books on new and related subjects. If you have an
idea for a book, please contact us at
proposals@schifferbooks.com

Schiffer Books are available at special discounts for bulk purchases for sales promotions or premiums.
Special editions, including personalized covers, corporate imprints, and excerpts can be created in
large quantities for special needs. For more information contact the publisher.

In Europe, Schiffer books are distributed by
Bushwood Books
6 Marksbury Ave.
Kew Gardens
Surrey TW9 4JF England
Phone: 44 (0) 20 8392 8585; Fax: 44 (0) 20 8392 9876
E-mail: info@bushwoodbooks.co.uk
Website: www.bushwoodbooks.co.uk

Other Schiffer Books by the Author:

Saving Squeak: The Otter Tale, 978-0-7643-3588-4, $14.99

Osprey Adventure, 978-0-7643-3684-3, $13.99

To my nieces and nephews, Brittni and
Kevin York and Braden and Finley Keats
                                            –JKC

To Billy and Teddy, with all my love
                                            –LJ

One fine afternoon, two boys bang through a screen door and rush into the front yard.

Moments later, a battered, brown football arcs silently through the air and spirals right into Matt's outstretched hands.

"Nice!" shouts Andy, "Now toss it...what the heck?"

Andy looks down. There, just below the rip in his jeans, is that a squirrel?

6

Sure enough, a little squirrel is climbing up his leg. Startled, Andy puts out his hand. With a wave of his thin furred tail, the squirrel leaps from Andy's knee to his wrist, scampers up his arm, across his chest, and hops onto his shoulder.

Peering directly at Andy through large, shiny, brown eyes, he wiggles his black whiskers. Andy peers back.

The squirrel's face is so close to Andy's that he can see short white, yellow, and brown hairs scattered across the animal's tiny, quivering face.

"Matt, what am I supposed to do now?" Andy quietly asks his laughing friend.

Matt, who can't stop giggling at the sight of the small squirrel and his surprised friend, isn't sure. He thinks the baby squirrel has been blown out of his nest during the morning's thunderstorm. Or, perhaps the mother squirrel had been moving her babies to a new, safer nest when she saw a snake and the baby fell to the ground.

Either way, Matt figures, they'd better get this little guy some help. Cute as he is, Matt knows squirrels don't make good pets.

As the little squirrel nestles into the space between Andy's ear and shoulder, Matt wonders aloud: "Has he fallen out of a tree? Is he cold?"

Leaving Andy with the furry mammal on his shoulder, Matt sprints home.

11

Minutes later and still laughing, Matt returns with a medium-sized cardboard box. Since the squirrel's eyes are wide open, his tail is nearly filled out and curling over his back, and he is clearly able to leap, Matt guesses the squirrel is six to seven weeks old.

"Is your dog in the house?" Matt asks Andy, "We want to make sure the baby is safe while we look around the base of those trees. I'll bet we find his brother or sister on the ground."

With a gloved hand, Matt gently plucks the young squirrel from Andy's neck and places him in the box, which is too tall for him to tip over should he try to get out.

Finally, the squirrel allows the boy to pick him up. Matt places him in the box with the first squirrel. On soft, bunched-up old shirts, the hairy pair curls up together, squeaking and clicking softly, as if they recognize each other.

With the squirrels resting warmly and comfortably in the box, Matt and Andy search the rest of the yard to be sure no other babies are on the ground.

19

Since they find no other siblings, the boys begin searching for the squirrels' nest—either a drey made in a hollow tree or a football-shaped mass of twigs, leaves, and bark in the fork of a tree. A loud chattering in a tall, nearby hickory makes it simple enough. "There's the mother," notes Matt, pointing to the prattling squirrel, "You can see she's angry; look at the hair standing up on her back." Just above her, what is left of the nest is clearly visible.

Since it will take the mother squirrel at least two hours to rebuild her home, Matt and Andy leave the babies in the box at the base of the tree. "She'll come get them when the new nest is complete," explains Matt, "It's okay that we touched the babies; our scent will not stop the mother from taking them back to the nest. But, we do need to get out of her sight so that she can feel safe retrieving them."

Grabbing their football, Matt and Andy hurry back into the house, hoping the mother will quickly return for her babies. Stationing themselves with binoculars at the front window, they watch the mother squirrel busily trip up and down the tree carrying brown leaves and small twigs in her mouth as she reconstructs the nest.

Once the nest is to her liking, the mother squirrel skips down the tree to the lowest branch. She sits up straight on her haunches and twitches her bushy tail quickly. She hangs upside down on the limb, then scurries headfirst down to the bottom of the tree before leaping mightily onto the edge of the box.

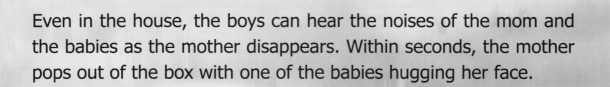

Even in the house, the boys can hear the noises of the mom and the babies as the mother disappears. Within seconds, the mother pops out of the box with one of the babies hugging her face.

A moment later, she re-emerges from the nest by herself. With a flick of her fluffy grey tail, she dashes daringly along the thin branches and darts back down the tree, clearly prepared to rescue her second baby.

Without stopping, she bustles back inside the high-sided container and scuttles out with the other baby around her face. Again, she races back up the tree to put the baby back into the nest.

Imagining the three squirrels gleefully clicking and barking about their happy reunion in their secure nest, Matt and Andy burst into cheer.

"Time to start the second half," Andy says with a laugh to Matt, and the boys head out to finish their game.

If you find an animal in need, you should seek help from a licensed wildlife rehabilitator, like Christina Clark. If the animal must be handled, use caution and wear gloves.

Thanks to Christina Clark for helping the author and illustrator ensure the accuracy of information in this book. Chris helps raise and release injured and orphaned wildlife. She has also become a valuable resource for other rehabilitators. Care of individual wild animals is a wonderful, but expensive, undertaking. To help Chris continue her work, the author donates a portion of the royalties from sale of this book to Chris' Squirrels & More. To learn more, visit **www.squirrelsandmore.com.**